Cabin

The Cabin

By

D W MORRIS

Cabin

Printed in the United States of America and United Kingdom

www.titanpublishinghouse.com

Titan InKorp LTD © is registered by the UK ISBN agency on the international ISBN Agency's Publisher Database

ISBN- 978-1-78520-027-4

Cabin

Contents

Cabin

By

D W MORRIS

Chapter 1

The taste of sick was still lingering inside David's mouth. He had been sick from a full day of drinking yet again. The loss of his wife weighed David down. She was a part of David's life he could not do without. His skin was turning yellow as his favourite bourbon was slowly killing him.

David ran himself a hot, steaming bath, while his favourite song was playing on his CD player. 'Love Me Tender'. This was David and his wife's song. They played it at their wedding. "I miss you," David cried as he looked up to the ceiling.

David starred at his kitchen knife he'd placed at the side of his bath tub. "I'll be with you soon." As tears fell from David's face, like a mini waterfall, goose bumps filled David's entire body. The depression was too much for David to bear.

David slowly stepped into the bath, wearing his clothes. He laid back and looked up to the ceiling yet again, his tears still streamed out of his eyes. David then took a deep breath as his yellow hand picked up his kitchen knife. As he paused, he cried out again. "It won't be long now my love." Then David sliced across his right wrist, the knife going through his skin like it was going through butter. The water in the bath tub soon changed from clear to red within seconds. The pain only lasted seconds, as David laid back, waiting to be by his wife's side, once again.

As he lay there, waiting, his head went under the water, until a figure appeared, wearing a long black cloak. His skin was a very pale complexion his fingers dirty and thin. As the pale man look down at David, a voice could be heard in the distance, as David's vision was getting darker.

"DAD!" called the voice again and again. Then, the pale man reached out to David and touched him. Suddenly, David was no longer in his bath tub.

The sun was shining as the birds in the lovely, green tree, sang. David couldn't ask for a better day. David was throwing a football to his son Greg, as his daughter Sarah and wife Mary were sitting on the hill next to the picnic basket.

"This is the life," David said to himself. This was how things were before David dream became a living nightmare.

The smell of burning flesh was over powering. The sky filled with red. The screams of pain echoed the entire area. David could see little strange beings, tormenting the people who were in bloody cages. Some other creatures were putting their filthy hands inside the screaming and scared people's mouths and other holes, pulling their inside out within minutes and laughing as they did so.

The heat was unbearable as the sweat was burning into David's body. He knew he would not see his wife here. The screams were not stopping and it was becoming deafening. David felt as he had been here a long time. As he looked at his scarred body, he then realised he had been. Flashbacks of days gone by, started to haunt him.

Flashes of a tall man with his face torn to shreds and pitch black eyes, with blood dripping from his muscular body. He stood at nine feet tall, with a bunch of chains, whipping David constantly for days. However, these were no ordinary chains as their touch would burn the flesh. David screamed for help as the creature laughed at David. He knew then, his screaming was helpless. David tried to blank out the pain, which was easier said than done. He tried to recall that summer's day with his family.

That's when darkness came across David and he saw men in masks looking down from above him.

"Clear," said one of the masked men. David was soon starting to see the light again, as a sudden, sharp shock went through his body. That's when the light grew brighter and David fell asleep.

"Dad," said a male voice. David slowly opened up his eyes to see a guy standing there, with dark wavy hair and scruffy stubble, wearing biker gear. As David blinked he realise it was his son, Greg, standing at the side of the bed.

"Greg, where am I?" David slowly spoke as he tried to focus on his son.

"You're in the hospital, Dad. You were in a bad way. Luckily the doctors managed to save you," replied David's concerned son, Greg. As a man in a white coat approaches David's bed.

"I'm Doctor Shepard, Mr. Steel. I'm the doctor who worked on you when you came in. You're lucky your son got to you when he did," said the Doctor.

"What do you mean?" David replied confused.

"Your son found you lying in your bath tub. He helped pull you out and called for ambulance" Doctor Shepard said softly.

"We need to keep you in for a while to tend to those stiches and help with the liver failure," said Doctor Shepard.

"Where's your sister, Greg?" asked David who was starting to feel very tired from the drugs he was on.

"She said she didn't want to see you this way. She is very upset with what has happened,

Dad. You know, she hasn't been the same since mum was murdered," Greg replied sadly.

"We're going to keep you in for couple days, then you'll be free to go home," Dr. Shepard said with a big smile on his face.

"I've got to go Dad," said Greg "I'm going to see Sarah, try convinces her to leave the house, it's not good for her to stay in all the time."

Greg left the room and so did the Doctor. David laid back and let the drugs do their job as he drifted softly into a deep sleep.

Chapter 2

"HELP ME!" screamed a very scared female voice. Her hair was covered in blood as her face was split open. She had been attacked and was laying there in a very bad way.

"Why?" said the female. That's when David realised it was his wife Mary, laying there. He froze. He couldn't even move to help her up. "WHAT THE FUCK IS GOING ON?" David screamed.

David then seen himself looking into a mirror above a skin. With his bald head and goatee all covered in his wife's blood. His old worn face staring, looking puzzled to what had just happen. As he moved his hands from the sink, the blood instantly stained everything he touched.

He washed his face hoping to wake up. He then looks into the mirror again to see the hideous creature he seen before with the chains looking back at him with its pitch black eyes and its grisly grin. It opened its mouth and dark blood came pouring out, with its worn, red teeth showing. With an eerie tone it spoke. "You will be back to me soon, David."

That's when heat came from the mirror and David's face started to burned, then melt, as the whole room ignited into flames. David screamed in agonising pain.

"DAD!" shouted Greg as he saw his Dad screaming in his sleep, shaking violently in the bed, rubbing his arms as if something was causing him great discomfort.

"Wake up!" Greg started to get worried looking around.

"Help!" shouted Greg as he started to panic. The doctor ran in with two nurses, who rushed to David's bed side. David then woke up and gasped for breath, as if he had his head under water for too long.

"Mr. Steel, are you okay?" Asked the concerned Doctor as he looked on his clip board.

"Where am I?" replied a very confused David as he was looking around the room which was unfamiliar to him.

"You're in the hospital. We told you this yesterday," replied his worried son.

"I must have had a bad dream," David said with fear in his eyes.

"What was it about?" asked Greg.

"Nothing really. Just a stupid nightmare. It must be the side effects of these drugs I'm taking," David said, but Greg knew there was more to it.

"Where's your sister, Sarah?" asked David.

"She said this place reminded her too much of mum and it hurts too much, but she said she'll pick you up, when you're ready to leave," replied Greg.

****

The days went by, as David sat and stared outside to the hospital garden. The rain poured and the sky was dark, no one could be seen outside. The sound of rain tapping the glass, was soothing to David.

David then noticed a man outside in the rain, standing looking directly at him. David moved nearer to the window to get a closer look. That's when the strange figure lowered something from his long black coat, as steam rose when the rain touch the man. David froze, as he noticed the man lower a set of chains. David rub his eyes and when he opened them again, he seen the monster again, but this time breathing against the window with blood smeared against it. It had moves about fifty yards in a matter of seconds.

"WHAT DO YOU WANT FROM ME?" David shouted with fear in his voice.

"Your soul!" replied the beast with an evil grin on his torn face.

David's son, Greg walks in to see his Dad shaking with terror, looking at the window.

"Dad... what's the matter?" Greg asked with curiosity. David turned to him with fear in his face and then looks back at the window to notice the monster had vanished.

"Nothing son, just tired, that's all," David spoke with a hint of anxiety in his voice.

"Sure you're okay?" pushed Greg, unconvinced by his father's response.

"I'm sure Son, don't worry about me," David reassured Greg. "I'm feeling great and cannot wait to get out of this room and get home."

"Well, Sarah and I have been talking. We're going to take you away. Would you like that?" Asked Greg.

"Where?" asked David. As he slowly sat up in his bed.

"The cabin," replied Greg. "Mum use to love it there." Greg then sat on the side of the bed.

"That she did," said David, with a hint of glee in his eye. As he took a swig of his water and knocking back painkillers.

****

The next day David was released from hospital and was waiting for the arrival of his daughter, Sarah. As he waiting outside with an umbrella, the rain was still pouring down as it has been for the past few weeks. David was still having visions. This time it was his wife watching from across the street, with blood dripping down her white wedding dress. He heard her speak.

"Why David? Why did you do it?" She asked.

"I did it so I can be with you again," replied David, as a tear fell from his cheek.

That's when a girl pulled up with long brown hair, freckles and big bright blue eyes. It was Sarah. She tooted her horn on her red Corsa but David was still glaring at the other side of the road.

"Dad," said Sarah but David did not respond. She looked at him and noticed he was glaring into thin air.

"DAD!" shouted Sarah as David fell out of his trance and he rubbed his eyes.

"Oh, Hello, Sarah dear. You okay, sweetheart?" David said with a muddled look upon his face.

"I'm okay. You were looking a little lost there, Dad. Sure you're okay?" Sarah asked baffled. She could see there was something bothering her father.

"Just tired love," replied David, as he looked worn out from the treatment in the hospital and the medication he was on.

"Hope you're ready for our little trip. Maybe you will tell us what's up, and the truth this time," said Sarah. "You know we are worried about you. Things haven't been the same since..."

"Your mother, I know" David said, as he finished Sarah sentence.

"I think this trip will help us all out, to be honest, Dad," said Sarah with excitement in her voice. "It's what we all need."

"Your right love. I'm really looking forward to it," David said. But Sarah did not look convinced.

Chapter 3

The family arrived at the cabin. With beautiful flower baskets hanging from each side of the door with green window sills and a gold sign saying office, it was just like they remembered. This place brought a smile to Sarah's face.

"I'll go inside and get the keys to the cabin," Sarah said as she looked at her father. She got out the red Corsa and headed towards the lodge. She opened up the bright coloured door to see an old lady sitting behind the desk, doing some paper work. The lady looked to be in her late sixties and looked a little worn. You could instantly tell this lady had been here a very long time.

"Pippa. Is that you?" Sarah said with excitement.

"Sarah dear. Oh my God, how long has it been?" Pippa said as she put on her old, brown glasses.

"Over fifteen years now. Oh how we have missed this place," said Sarah with a smile upon her face.

"How's the family? I was so sorry to hear about your mother too. She was such a lovely woman," Pippa said with a sad tone in her voice.

"It's been hard, but we're slowly getting there," replied Sarah. "It will take time."

"It will dear. It took a while when Harold died. Time is a healer. So, did they catch the guy who did it?" asked the old lady.

"We know who did it, but there was no evidence to prove it," Sarah replied sharply, as she looked out the lodge window. She could see her brother and father sitting in the car, not even looking at each other.

"Well I hope justice will find its way to whoever did it," said Pippa.

"It will, sooner rather than later," Sarah said angrily. That's when Pippa handed over the keys to the cabin with a concerned look in her eyes.

Sarah took the keys and headed out to the car. She looked in the car to see her father, looking at a photo of his wife, Mary. She climbed into the car and looked at her father once again with mixed emotions.

"We've got to drive down to the bottom of the road, then it's on foot from there. We got our old cabin," said Sarah.

"No problem love. The exercise will do me good," replied David.

"How far is the walk? I can't remember, it's been so long," said Greg as he took a drag of his cigarette.

"You need to give that up, bro," said Sarah, as she was appalled with her brother addiction.

"One day, maybe," Greg spoke as he took another deep drag of his cigarette.

They drove down to the bottom of the road, which led to a big car park. As they got out of the vehicle, they looked at the forest which covered miles of land scape. The rain had eased off, but it wasn't the weather they came for. It was a break for the family to get together after all the years they had been apart.

They headed into the forest to get to the cabin, which was a twenty minute walk. The silence made Sarah feel uneasy, so she tried to break it.

"Shit weather again. At least it's stopped raining for the time being," Sarah said.

"I just can't wait to get to the cabin and get the fire going," replied Greg.

They made their way down the pebbled path. Once they turned the corner, they saw the old cabin, which they hadn't visited in many years. They all paused and took a long at the cabin. It was a little more worn than what they remember it.

"The place looks different," spoke Greg.

"Well, we haven't been here in a long time. Of course it's going look different, you twat," laughed Sarah.

They headed into the cabin. They looked inside to see it had a modern look. It looked all new to Sarah and Greg but David had a look of familiarity on his face.

They decided to make some food and watch a film together, that's when they noticed David had gone.

"Where's Dad?" Asked Greg as he was looking around.

"He went outside, I think," replied Sarah.

"Thought we were spending quality time together," Greg replied nastily, looking at Sarah.

"Lose the attitude dick head. He has only gone for fresh air," said Sarah, with an angry tone.

Greg went outside to see his father standing looking at a small tree. Which stood out from the rest of the forest. It had strange marking on it.

"What you doing Dad?" Asked Greg.

"Nothing Son, just thinking," answered David, still morning his wife's death. As a single tear fell from David's eye.

They opened the door and both headed back inside.

"Where's your sister?" Asked David, as he looked around.

"She is right behind you," replied Greg.

As David turn he caught a glimpse of Sarah with an ash tray, as she smashed it onto her father's head, knocking him down to the ground.

"We want the truth you sick fucker!" shouted Sarah.

"I'll go get the chains!" exclaimed Greg, as he hurried off.

Greg left the room. David's head was gashed open, as he lay there, helpless. The room was spinning as David tried to refocus his blurred vision. That's when he noticed in the corner of the room the outline of a tall figure, lower chains yet again from his long black coat.

"Soon," said the eerie man from the corner of the room. "Soon and then I can claim what is rightfully mine."

Chapter 4

David was in a dark room. He lifts his head. He notices his two children standing over him, as he was chained to a wooden chair.

"Why, you fucking sick twat?" Shouted an angry Sarah.

As blood dripped from David's head he responded.

"What do you mean?" David said as he spat blood out of his mouth.

"What you did to mum! You know what we're talking about!" Greg shouted directly at his father's face. Then he lashed at his face with the chain, breaking David's nose and the blood poured out.

"WHY??" demanded Sarah, as she slapped her father round his face. "Your filth, you disgusting man. You're not my father, I don't know who the fuck you are." She was outraged.

The son then picked up a hammer and nails, looking at his father.

"I'm going to make you suffer like you did to Mum," Greg said holding up the hammer as he placed the tip of the nail upon his hands. With one big swing, the nail was sent straight through David's hands and into the wooden chair. David screamed in pain. Greg then moves to the other hand. He then bashes a nail into the other hand.

"Feeling helpless aren't you...David" Greg smirked. As Greg continued to hammer the nails further into the chair arm. The blood trickled from David's hand's down to the wooden floor of the cabin.

"Just tell us why? We know you did it!" Sarah spoke, standing back watching her brother smashing the hammer onto David's knuckles. He was in pain and it was clear to see it from the expressed on his face.

David then started to see the monster standing behind Sarah. He was enjoying watching David in pain. Greg then grabs his carpenter knife and starts slices at David's face slowly carving at his nose.

"Are you enjoying this?" David shouted as a spit of blood came out of his mouth.

"No, we don't enjoy this, but justice should be dealt and the waste of space cops, won't do shit," replied an angry Greg.

"More!" said the creature standing back, with an evil smile upon his torn up face.

David glared straight at the creature. Then David smirked. His kids left the room as it was becoming too much for them.

"This is getting crazy," Sarah said terrified. She was becoming very anxious. She wanted to make her dad pay for what he had done to their mother but this was just too much.

"We need to finish him off and bury him in the ground out back" Greg said stomping up and down, fuming. Greg was very close to his mother and wanted to make his father pay. They knew that their mother was trying to leave their father. That's when Sarah remember the time when Mary told her about another man, called Liam.

She could remember it clearly. She was sitting in their old house, in the kitchen with her mother. "Don't be mad with me Sarah, but I'm leaving your father."

"Why Mum?" Sarah replied, as she looked worried.

"Your father hasn't been the same since you and Greg were children," Mary explained, looking down at the floor. "I've also met someone else."

Sarah had a look of betrayal on her face as she sipped her cup of tea.

"I'm sorry love, but I just can't keep living a lie anymore. Your father has a violent streak in him." Mary continued, holding her hands against her head, brushing back her hair.

"Has he been violent to you?" Sarah asked concerned for her mother.

"More times than I can count. Every time a guy spoke to me, your father would lash out," Mary said with fear in her eyes. Sarah could see her mother had enough. Sarah got up and hugged her mother.

"It's okay. If you feel this way, then maybe you should leave," Sarah softly spoke as she wiped away her mother's tears. She was sad for her mother. She just wanted her to be happy.

"When are you leaving, Mum?" Sarah inquired.

"Tonight, Sarah. As soon as your dad leaves for work. I've already packed all my bags. He'll be picking me up from the local shop at six." Mary was excited but yet still a little worried at the same time.

Sarah went and started doing the washing up. She looked outside to see her father in the garden, going about his business.

"Do you think dad has any ideas?" Sarah asked while she was cleaning a cup with number one dad written upon it."

"No, Sarah, I don't think so. I just need this to go smoothly. As soon as Liam and I find somewhere, I will get in touch. But for now, it's going to be quiet for a while. Then after a few weeks, I'll file for divorce"

Sarah didn't realise her father was so bad. As kids the family were all happy. Spending a lot of quality time together. Family holidays to the cabin happened annually. The days at the park as Greg and David played football. While Sarah and

Mary made the food up for everyone. The family were so happy. But that's when Sarah remember a little incident back when she was around seven years old.

She remembered a man in a sports hoodie speaking to her mother. All she remembered was he had a big smile on his face. He was pretty tall too. Taller than an average man. He was around the seven foot mark. That's when David came out looking very shifty. Coming through the forest holding a hammer and chasing the tall guy away.

"I'm going to kill you," shouted David.

How did Sarah forget this? The tall guy always rented the cabin next door too. She remembered him. She tried to remember his name. He ran away as he didn't want trouble with her father. David pointed at Mary with an angry look. All she remembered after that was, she never seen that guy again.

"What was his name?" Sarah asked herself?

Chapter 5

Their father was bleeding out in the dark room of the cabin. Sitting there chained up helplessly. David then started coughing the blood from out of his mouth. The very lightly lit room started flicker as the bulb was on its way out. David noticed the monster standing in front of him yet again.

"What... the fuck... do you want from... me?" questioned David as he struggled to even speak the words.

"Your soul...as you took mine," the eerie creature said as his face grew closer to David. David could smell death upon him.

David started to looked puzzled. He didn't know who or what this creature was, or what it was going to do. All he knew was he was scared and helpless.

The monster then put its hands on David's hands. As the touch burned David and his skin started to blister, David's hands felt like his skin was melting.

"I've got HELL of a lot more for you, Wife Beater," said the monster with an evil expression. The pitch black eyes kept showing flashes of David and his violent ways.

"I know all. I see all," whispered the monster.

"Are you...the devil?" asked David as blood was still covering his terrified face.

"Oh no, David," said the monster in his spine-chilling tone. "I'm revenge in its physical form."

"Please, no more," David pleaded, as he could not bear to look into its eyes any longer.

"I'm only just starting," replied the grisly creature. "Oh, by the way, your whore of a wife says hi."

David started to get angry trying to escape the chains holding him to the chair and the nails still stuck into his blister hands.

"I'M GOING TO FUCKING KILL YOU!" Screamed David with such rage in his face.

The door swung open and his children came in. Greg ran up to David and smashed him across the face.

"SHUT UP!" demanded Greg and he took another swing at his weaken father.

"You're going to pay for what you did to Mum," Sarah said. "And what you did to that tall guy who use to stay in the fucking cabin next door!" Sarah said in outrage.

"What you mean, Sarah?" asked Greg as he didn't know what she was talking about.

"HE KILLED HIM TOO!" Sarah shouted.

"You mean Neville?" said Greg. "He was freakily tall.

"Neville! Yes, that was his name," Sarah then replied.

"I seen you chasing him with a hammer saying you were going to kill him...didn't you...David?" Sarah questioned David.

Greg then went over to the tool box in the corner of the room. He took out the hammer back out from the tool box once again. He walked up to David and started lashing out at his knee caps.

"How does it feel?" Greg asked, as he continued to hit David.

"Let's take him around the back," Sarah says. "I can't take any more of this shit"

She knew what they were doing was wrong but she had to make things right as it wasn't fair that he wasn't punished for killing their mother.

Greg then pushed David into a wheelbarrow and pushes him out the back of the cabin. They knew as it was autumn, no one would be around. The night gave them cover too and now the rain had return it make it harder to see clearly. Greg then drag David to the spot he was looking at early.

"So, why were you looking at this spot then David?" Quizzed Greg but David did not respond.

Greg then starts to dig in the area David was looking at when they arrived earlier that day. That's when Greg discovered the remains of human bones.

"What the fuck?" Greg said looking a little spooked.

"You found him then?" Sarah asked. As she looked into the hole.

The remains were of that of a tall man. They soon realised that the father must have buried Neville in this spot.

"I knew it," Sarah stated. As they turned around, they noticed that David had gone. They both nervously turn around checking everywhere.

"He couldn't have gotten very far," said Greg as he was holding a shovel for protection.

"Let's head into the cabin. Maybe he has locked himself in there. And if so, we'll burn him in there," suggested Sarah, as she was hiding behind Greg.

They headed up to the cabin door and turn the door knob and when it opened, they saw a blood trail heading into the kitchen.

"Stay behind me, Sarah," instructed Greg, who was trying to look after his younger sister.

They slowly head into the kitchen and that's when all the lights went out.

"Shit!" Said Sarah as she was now very spooked.

They slowly headed to the back room where Greg knew there was a torch in the tool box. As they entered the room, they were very weary. Greg, still holding the shovel just in case he need to put down David. Sarah then ran over to the tool box picking up the torch. She switched it on but did not come on at first. She became worried, so she gives it a little tap and then the light came on. As she shone the torch towards the door, they saw their father standing there, looking directly at them with blood covering his whole body.

"Time to discipline you spoilt little shits," David said. As he ran towards them holding a hammer. Greg swung the shovel, knocking David down to the floor and starts stamping on him. David was then knocked out yet again. The brother and sister then decide they had no choice but to burn him inside. They find the fuel around the back and head back inside to see David still lying there. They pour the petrol over David and all over the room.

"Mum will punish you when you see her," Sarah said as she was cried.

Greg then lights a match and then threw to the ground as it lights up like a bonfire on Guy Fawkes Night. They both head outside to watch the place go up in a blaze.

Chapter 6

Sarah listens to the radio as she is in her home and lying in the bath. She was suddenly surprised to what she hears.

'Fire fighters were at Woodies forest cabins, as one of the cabins went up in a blaze tonight. No bodies were found inside the cabin, but the remains of a Neville Morgan were found just outside. Forensics say the remains are over ten years old, maybe even longer. There was no evidence of foul play but police are looking for a brother and sister, Sarah and Gregory Steel and their father David Steel. As they were the family renting this cabin at the time of the blaze, I'm Emily Green, back to you guys in the studio'

Sarah jumps up and wraps a towel around her and heads downstairs to where Greg had fallen asleep on the couch. Sarah woke him up.

"He isn't dead" Sarah shakily said.

"What?" Greg says confused as he is still half a sleep.

"I'm going to get dressed, then we're going to look for him" she said as she made her way back up the wooden staircase.

Sarah went into her bedroom and headed towards the wardrobe. She slipped on a pair of legging and a sports jumper and jumped into her pair of trainers. She headed back downstairs and noticed that Greg had disappeared. She walks into the kitchen but still could not find her brother.

Where is he? Thought Sarah angrily, as she continued to search the house. She had only been gone a few minutes. She headed towards the front door. That's when she noticed it was opened a little. When she reached the door, she pushed it open further. The lights from the town could be seen but no sounds could be heard, as it was the early hours of the morning.

Where is that twat? Sarah thought to herself once again. She scratched her head in confusion before she turned back around and heads back into the house. She shut the front door behind herself. She heard a plate smash, coming from the kitchen. She jumped as chills filled her whole body, suddenly she felt cold.

"GREG!" Shouted Sarah as she slowly moved towards the kitchen. But there was no response.

"Is that you?" She called out. "Come on, this isn't funny." Sarah was getting very worried now. She pushes open the door. She put her head around the corner. SMASH! Another plate hit the floor and then she notices the ginger cat on the kitchen counter top next to the plate rack.

"You little shit," Sarah said holding her hand on her chest. She was extremely jumpy but relieved it was just a cat. Where was her brother?

She then headed back into the living where it was warmer with the wood fire glowing and heating up the room. She heads over to the table and picks up her mobile phone and then dialled her brother's number. She could hear the ring from his phone coming from upstairs. She ran up there quickly, hoping that her brother decided to go to his room. She knocks on his bedroom door.

"Greg!" Sarah said. As she was still knocking on his door. The door opens a tad. She peeked her head in to find her brother hanging from the light fixture on the ceiling.

"NO!!!" She screamed out in horror, as she turned and ran back downstairs. As she ran, she tripped and fell, landing on her face. She lifted herself up, feeling a buzzing sensation in her head. She looked up and that's when she noticed her father, all burnt, looking down at her. His face was blistered over and there were marks on his hands from where the nails were hammer into him. His clothing all black from the soot from the fire. He must have been in there a while before escaping. He made his way over to Sarah.

"You've been a naughty girl, Sarah. Like your brother, this will not go without you being punished," David said as he headed towards his daughter. He was holding a meat cleaver in his hand. He swung it up to the air and sliced off Sarah's hand. Sarah screamed in agony, as the blood poured out, she grabs the stump with her other hand, trying to stop the bleeding.

"Don't like it when it's you, do you, Sarah?" Grinned David. She knew her father was a monster and now he was showing it. He then grabs her leg and starts dragging her into the lounge.

"Want to know what I had done to your slut of a mother? She was the only woman I have ever loved. It was an accident. She just got in the way. It was supposed to be that prick Liam, I was going to kill," David said, as he kicked his daughter in the stomach. "But she had to jump in the way."

David then started to cry and headed over to the alcohol on the table next to the phone. Sarah was still on the floor holding her arm

"I got this very knife and I swung for him. Your mother then tried to stop me and I...I caught her in the throat. He tried to stop me and we ended up on the floor fighting, so I reached out for the phone in this spot and hit him over the head several times and that's when the shouting from him stopped." David took a gulp from the bourbon bottle.

"I then took their bodies to the woods and burned them," David continued.

"Don't worry my daughter, the family will be together soon. Just like the good old days," grinned David, as he took another swig.

He walks over to Sarah while still holding the meat cleaver and put it on her face.

"Your mother will be so disappointed in you for what you did, Sarah," David said softly.

"What about... you? What you did to her and Liam and Neville? You're not even... human," replied Sarah who was about to pass out from her blood loss. David raises his hand as he was about to slash Sarah neck, when suddenly, the police barge into the house and see David holding the knife.

"Put down your weapon," the police officer said firmly, his gun pointed at David.

He then tries to take a swing at Sarah, but the officer shot David in the arm putting him down to the ground. The officer headed over to

Sarah to see if she is okay. He puts a call through on his walkie-talkie.

"We need assistance at the Steel residence. We have two people down, a young female in her twenties, who appears to be missing a hand. The male was taken down as he tried to take another swing at the female with a kitchen meat cleaver. He appears to have serious burns all over his body," said the office into his walkie-talkie. As he checked Sarah's pulse, it was becoming very faint.

"My brother is up stairs, dead," Sarah struggled to say before she passed out. The officer called for backup one more time.

Chapter 7

A blue flashing light pulled up outside the house of the Steel family. The rain was still pouring down like there was no tomorrow. They rushed inside with the ambulance team and two police officers. But when they got inside, they were not expecting to find what they did.

Blood covered the walls from top to bottom. The room lit up red from the blood on the light bulb. The officer, who first came to help was laying on the ground, ripped open. As if he was attacked by a beast of some sort.

The girl was in the position of the crucifixion, nailed to the wall with the words, *Bad girl* written in blood above her head. The scene was too much for the officers, as they all started to vomit.

But where was David? He was nowhere to be seen.

The officers continued to search the house to find Greg hanging up in his bedroom. The police put out an A.P.B on David. As he was now the most wanted man in the entire area.

"We have to find this guy. No one should be free who would do this to their own daughter," said a sickened police office to one of the ambulance members, as they slowly lowering Sarah from the wall. But what the police did not know was, David wasn't just hiding from the them. He was also hiding from something a lot worse.

******

Across the town, is a place where the homeless dwell. Where abandoned buildings fill the small area, which was once a blooming town at one point. David was hiding inside the tallest of all the major buildings. The smell of rotten food and litter polluted the air. There were small fires in hallways so the homeless could try keep warm, as walls had fallen down and there was big, gaping holes in the roof. David was alone, cold and wounded.

Why am I not dead? thought David, as he rubbed himself to keep warm, as rain drops coming in through the hole in the roof, kept hitting him in the face.

"I know you are here," said the now familiar weird, eerie voice, yet again.

"Leave me alone," pleaded David, who as curled up in the corner. The creature leaned around the doorway and with a piecing look, stared at David who didn't want to return the look.

"We are not yet finished yet, David. Have you remembered who I am yet?" The creature said as it gradually inched closer. He grabbed

David around the neck. David screamed as the touch burnt his skin.

"We have a long time to play," said the creature, who then began to laugh as the mere torture of David pleased him. "I won't let you die so easy. And don't worry about your daughter and the police, I left them a nice little gift in the house when you snuck out" grinned the monster.

"Who...are...you?" David asked slowly, as he was still being choked.

"Isn't it obvious?" Replied the tall beast of a monster. "You took my soul, now I'm going to torture yours, and then take it." The creature, who was clearly over powering David, just laughed out loud.

"You think you are safe in this building?" asked the creature, who let David down. David tried to catch his breath as he tried standing, only to fail and fall again. He was weak and he was only going to get weaker.

"Do you think you are really in a building?" The monster asked David and soon as David looked up, he was back in the burning cage he was once in. The screams once again echoed as David tried to cover up his ears. It was too much to bear. The sky lit up red as if it were on fire. The smell was unbearable. David had noticed that his body was healed. His scars and burns had gone, the wounds on his hands where the nails had gone through, vanished.

"What the...?" David was baffled. 'How did this happen?'

"You didn't think I was going to let you rot so quickly, did you?" Asked the monster who was looking at the wall with skulls burnt into it.

"You think we will get peace now David?" the monster continued to grill David, as he was enjoying tormenting him.

"WHO ARE YOU?" Demanded David, as he squared up to the creature. The creature then stopped looking at the wall and turned around. Suddenly he resembled David.

"I'm what you will become," replied the monster, as it grinned. David was taken aback by this and collapsed on to the floor.

"Did you really think your family would try to kill you?" asked the monster curiously. David didn't respond.

"Your kids don't even know what you did to their mother!" It continued taunting David. "Did you really think you killed your wife and her lover?"

David still didn't speak.

"Do you really think your wife could ever do that to you?" it asked in a low, spiteful whisper.

"Why?" cried David holding his hands against his face as his tears fell.

"To control and break you," said the monster. "I have a mission and I need your body. I will become what you wouldn't ever dream about. I will look after your family…"

"MY FAMILY ARE DEAD!" Shouted David, as he rose to his feet.

"In your mind they are, But in reality they are sitting by your bedside, as we speak" it said laughing.

"What you mean? I saw them die!" David replied, feeling confused by what the creature was saying to him.

"You see what I want you to see," grinned the creature, as it grabbed David and then threw him up against the wall.

"Leave me alone!" Demanded David as he got back to his feet.

"I'm going to make sweet love to your wife and then fuck her to death," laughed the monster as it began to pull out its chains again. It swung the chains at David, tearing at his face. David fell to the ground and then his meat cleaver fell to the floor. David then tried to reach it.

"Go on David, pick it up. It won't kill me," said the monster, as it stood back so that David could pick it up. David then stood up, holding the meat cleaver firmly in his hand.

"Do your best David," ordered the monster as it held its hands up.

"I will," David replied as he held the blade of the cleaver up to his own throat and started hacking away at his own skin.

"NO!!!" Screamed the monster in a terrifying cry. It tried to stop David and as David fell to the ground, he had a smile on his face,

knowing that he was finally free of this demon.

Then Darkness.

Chapter 8

David started to see some light shining through his eye lids. He slowly opened them to see a white room. He looked around with his blurred vision to see three people standing either side of him.

"Relax, David," said a soft, familiar voice. David's vision became clear and to his surprise, his wife and two kids were sitting beside him.

"You okay, Dad?" Asked Greg, who had his usually bike leathers on.

"Still riding that death trap?" David asked with a smile on his face.

"Yes Dad, you know me and bikes," replied Greg with a relieved laugh. Sarah then leans over and started to hug her father.

"Where am I anyways?" Asked David, as he slowly started to sit up.

"St Margret's asylum. You were in a bad way Dad, but the doctor thinks you will be back to normal in no time," explained Sarah as she then gave her father a kiss on the cheek.

"The doctor will be in soon to see you, love," Mary told David, as she handed him a glass of water. "And this time, will you take your medication. We don't want you having another bad episode again," Mary pleaded with David.

David took the glass of water and the two pills then swallowed them.

"There you go," said Mary with a smile on her face. "That wasn't too bad, was it dear?"

David had a big smile on his face. He was happy that it was all in his head. He knew now that he must get on with his life. But first, he needed to get better and leave the asylum. He knew it would take time.

A little worn old man walks in. He was wearing a shirt, tie and a long white coat.

"Hello, Mr. Steel. I'm Dr. Backlund. How are you feeling today?" asked the doctor with a welcoming smile.

"I'm feeling a little shaky but other than that, I'm feeling great. I've got my family here with me. What more do I need?" Said a positive David.

"That's good to know. We're going to have to keep you in for a couple more weeks for observation, but I think everything will be fine from now on, Mr. Steel." This sounded promising to David and it gave him hope.

"I've got to go now, but I will be back in five minutes," said Dr. Backlund.

Greg then got up and looked out the window, then suggest an idea to help his family.

"Hey Dad. When you do finally get out this place, how about a holiday?" asked Greg who was very enthusiastic as he headed back towards the bed.

"That sounds great son. Where did you have in mind?" replied David as he was drinking his water.

"I know. How about the cabin we use to go to as kids?" Sarah suggested as she looked at her mother.

"That's a great idea," Mary agreed. "I wonder if Pippa still works there."

"Oh yes. It'll be lovely to see her," said Sarah.

The family then sat around the bed playing their favourite board game. David hadn't felt this happy in a long time. Things were looking up. Just to see the smiles of his wife and two children brought joy to David.

"I've got this book for you to read Dad," said Greg handing him a book he had taken out of his back pack.

"What is it?" Asked David, looking excited as David loved a good book.

"It's Hidden Darkness, by C J Austin. It's a good book. Might make you jump a little," laughed Greg.

"Can't wait to read it," David grinned as he took the book from Greg.

"I'm going to have to go, Dad," said Greg. "I've got a night shift tonight and I'm going to have to get some sleep before I leave, but I will visit you tomorrow and we can talk about what you think of the book." Greg got up and looked at his father. "I'm glad you're getting better. I've missed the real you," smiled Greg.

"Okay son, enjoy your shift and I'll see you tomorrow," smiled David. Greg then walked out of the room just leaving his mother and sister with his dad.

"I'm going to have to go too," said Sarah staring at her father with her deep blue eyes. She was a lawyer and was working on a big case.

"How come love?" Asked David.

"I'm working on a murder case. You must have heard of that guy who slaughter that entire family?" asked Sarah

"No, sorry love," David said without a clue as to what Sarah was talking about.

"Its big time for me and I don't want to be late," Sarah said as she got up and took her brief case from below the bed. She leaned over and kissed her father on the cheek.

"Bye love," David said. Sarah then walked out of the room.

"Want a coffee love?" asked Mary as she stood up.

"I'm okay, thanks," replied David as he looked at the front cover of the book. Mary headed to the door as it was still open. The doctor walked into the room, as soon as Mary left.

"Okay, David?" Asked the doctor.

"Yeah, I'm great. Just can't wait to go home," David replied with a huge grin on his face.

"I told you your family was okay, didn't I, David?" Said the doctor.

"Excuse me?" David asked all confused.

"When I was torturing and tormenting you," grinned the Doctor as he eyes started to become black and the room became very warm. "You didn't think I would let you go without a fight, did you?" Within the blink of an eye, the doctor took the form of the creature and started smothering David as he screamed for help, but his voice slowly disappeared and David's cries became helpless.

"I told you, your soul belongs to me," squealed the demon as it started to enter David's body.

A few minutes later, David's wife entered the room and looked at David sitting on the edge of the bed staring at the rain falling outside.

"What a day love. Can't wait for you to get home," said Mary as she moved beside David and put her arm around him. "How are you feeling now?"

"Like a new man," David smirked.

Cabin

By

D W MORRIS

Cabin

Published by Titan Publishing House